Manny's a Thief!

Tamar Books

Special thanks to the Rubashkin family, Atlanta's Beth Jacob community, and the Atlanta Scholars Kollel. Without their dedication to education and spiritual growth this book would not have been possible.

Manny's a Thief!

By Getzel

In the middle of the busy city, across from the green park where the oak tree stood, was a large apartment building. It was tall and narrow and had fifteen stories. Lots of people lived in it. There were tall people and short people, fat people and skinny people, young and old. The people were all very friendly with each other. Everybody liked everybody and everybody talked with everybody. But sometimes the people got a little too friendly and wanted to know a little too much about everybody else. The people who lived in this building were what you might call nosy. Sometimes they listened and repeated things that they should not have listened to and should not have repeated.

One day, Mrs. Golden and her grandson, David, were climbing the stairs to their fourth floor apartment. Mrs. Golden never took the elevator, she said she needed the exercise. They stopped to catch their breath at the top of the third flight. They were carrying bags of groceries so the trip was a bit tiring.

They were about to continue their journey up the next flight of stairs when Mrs. Golden thought she heard a voice coming from one of the apartments. She started listening more closely, but she really should have been minding her own business.

A muffled voice came from the hallway, "Mmmnys a eef."

Mrs. Golden's ears perked up. "What did they say? Who said that?"

"That was nothing, Grandma, come on..." said David as he started up the steps.

"No, no... I heard something..."

Mrs. Golden put her ear up to the door of the apartment that was right next to the stairway. All the doors had big numbers written on them. This door had the number 31-C. Now she could hear somewhat clearer. A rough voice was speaking, "Manny's a thief! Manny's a thief!"

Mrs. Golden jumped back. "Manny's a thief? That's awful!" thought Mrs. Golden out loud. "Why that bad man! Did you hear that, David? I can't believe it!"

"I think you misunderstood, Grandma," said David.

"I heard it with my own ears! Manny's a thief." Mrs. Golden was shocked. "But which Manny's a thief?" Mrs. Golden knew lots of Mannys.

"There's Manny who works at the bank on Thirty-ninth Street and there's Mr. Mannie who teaches school a few blocks away ... A school teacher, a thief? How could it be ..."

David kept tugging at his grandmother's side, "Grandma, Grandma, I think you misunder-stood..." But it was no use. Mrs. Golden was lost in her thoughts trying to think which Manny was the thief.

Just then Mrs. Overlander from the fifth floor came down the stairs.

Mrs. Overlander didn't take the elevator either — she had motion sickness and avoided moving objects completely.

"Psst! Mrs. Overlander!" whispered Mrs. Golden. "Have I got news for you!"

"We were on our way upstairs, minding our own business, when I happened to overhear that there's a terrible thief running loose around here! His name is Manny. Such a thief this Manny is. If I were you I'd lock my doors!"

"Grandma!" David tried to interrupt, but she immediately cut him off.

"Manny's a thief?" Mrs. Overlander shivered. Now Mrs. Overlander only knew of one Manny — the fix-it man who lived down in the basement, and she never trusted him in the first place. He had beady eyes, so she thought — the scoundrel! "I suspected it all along!" said Mrs. Overlander. And she scurried back upstairs to make sure she had locked her door.

As Mrs. Overlander reached her apartment door, she ran into Alex Morton, a retired doctor who still made occasional housecalls to his favorite patients, but mainly spent his time reading books and playing golf.

"Excuse me, Dr. Morton," Mrs. Overlander began, "but I thought you'd better know, Manny, the fix-it man, the man who lives down in the basement, is a dangerous thief! He's a menace and should be avoided! Lock your doors!"

Dr. Morton was surprised. Manny the fix-it man? "Well, come to think of it, a few things have been missing around my apartment... and Manny did come over just the other day to change some light bulbs... Well, what do you know? So he's the one who took my wife's gold ring!!! Thanks for the information. I'm going to the seventh floor to see Mrs. Kressler. She's ill and may need some help. I'll be sure to tell her not to call Manny." And Dr. Morton walked off.

Mrs. Overlander knocked on a few more of her neighbors' doors spreading the word that Manny, the fix-it man, was a terrible jewel thief — robbing everybody one by one. He couldn't be trusted. Hide your gold, silver, and fine crystal. THERE'S A THIEF AMONG US!!!

Well, since everyone in the apartment building talked with everyone else, within no time at all the word had spread, like wildfire! Wherever you went a group was gathered. Everyone was talking about how awful it was that Manny  the fix-it man was a hardened criminal.

"I heard he had a bad childhood, you know ... His father left home when Manny was three ... It's no wonder he turned out the way he did ..."

"I heard he has a drinking problem... Just the other day I saw him buying a bottle of wine ..."

"To think we trusted him and let him into our homes. We let him be around our children ... and he is a criminal! Thank Heaven we're all alive."

People talked about Manny the thief day and night. Around every corner another bit of juicy information could be learned. The story grew and Grew and GREW! Until ...

.... Manny the fix-it man turned one of those corners as he was making his rounds. Everyone stopped and stared as Manny began to walk down the corridor. Manny saw everyone and said hello. But nobody said hello back. Everyone just stared. Some shook their heads, others merely turned up their noses.

Then Manny turned another corner. The few people who were gathered around the elevator all scattered and ran back to their rooms and Manny heard everyone lock their doors. "What's the matter with everyone today?" thought Manny the fix-it man.

Manny then knocked on Mrs. Julio's door, 37-J. It was time to change her air filter. Mrs. Julio came to the door, but when she saw who it was her eyes grew wide and she screamed, "THIEF! You're not coming into my apartment! My son will come and change the filter from now on!" Then she slammed the door and bolted it shut.

Manny was left standing in the hallway, all alone.

"Why did she call me a thief?" Manny wondered. "I'm not a thief. I never stole anything... no wonder everyone's been acting so strangely, they must all think I'm a thief. What could I have done to make them think that?" Manny felt terrible. His feelings were hurt. He walked away from Mrs. Julio's door with his head down. "I'm ruined," he thought. "Now no one will trust me to fix anything. How will I make a living? I'm ruined ..."

Manny turned another corner and saw another group gathered, murmuring among themselves, whispering and snickering. There were bits of "Manny did this" and "Manny did that" coming from the conversation.

When Manny heard this he was about to cry. "They're talking about me! I can tell — they're spreading lies about me — LIES!" So Manny marched right up to the group and before they had a chance to run away, he demanded, "Why does everyone think I'm a thief? I'm not a thief! Who told you I was a thief?"

Everyone became silent and stared blankly at Manny. Then everyone started to point a finger at everyone else.

"Well, he told me ..."
"Well, I heard it from Simon ..."
"Well, Marge told me ..."
"Well, I heard it from ..."

At that point, David stepped forward. He had been listening to the entire conversation from around the corner. "I don't think you're a thief, Manny,"

David smiled. "If everyone will follow me, I think I can solve everything."

So everyone followed David.

They all paraded down the hallway. As people heard the excitement they all came out of their apartments one by one and joined the group. When they reached the end of the hallway David went up and knocked on the door that had 31-C written in large print.

A little boy answered and was surprised to see all the people staring at him, but when he saw his friend David he gave a big grin.

"Go put on your favorite hat!" David told the little boy. The little boy vanished.

Everyone was peeking into the apartment, looking around. Hanging from the ceiling was a bird cage. A colorful parrot sat perched up high.

Quick as a flash the little boy returned. He was now wearing his red fireman's hat. The hat had "CHIEF" written on it in tall, white letters.

"Everyone, this is my new friend, Manny Lamb. He moved in two weeks ago. He's going to be a fire chief when he grows up!" As those words came out of David's mouth, the bird that was in the cage began to caw:

"MANNY'S A CHIEF!"
"MANNY'S A CHIEF!"
"And that's Manny's pet parrot, Tricksy!" David finished.

Everyone was quiet.
"MANNY'S A CHIEF!" Tricksy cawed again.

Everyone turned to Manny the fix-it man. Then everyone started apologizing all at once. "We're so sorry. We didn't mean to hurt you. Please forgive us. It was just a misunderstanding."

Manny the fix-it man accepted everybody's apology, after all, it was just a misunderstanding. Manny wasn't a thief, Manny was a chief!

"This would never have happened if everyone would have stopped listening and repeating things when they should have been minding their own business," said David.

Everyone agreed. Spreading rumors was very bad and they would never do it again.

A few weeks later when Mrs. Golden was catching her breath at the top of the third flight, she thought she heard someone say, "Manny's a crook!" She looked around but didn't see anyone.

She thought for a moment and wondered, but then she shook her head and continued up the stairs ...